Write and draw and learn more about yourself in this book, you should. Fun, you will have. Heh heh.

JEDI ACADEMY

ATTACK OF THE JOURNAL

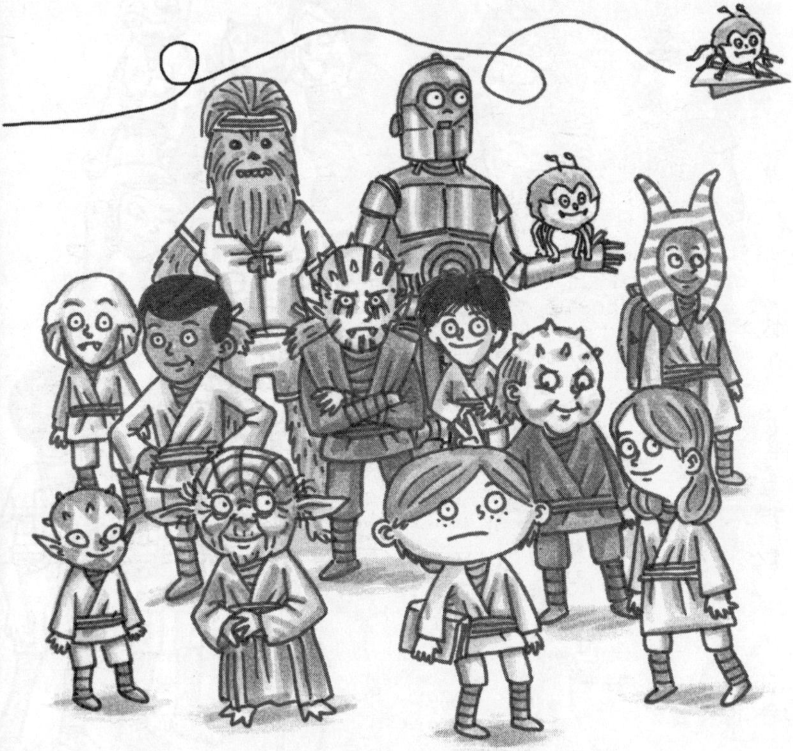

by *New York Times* Bestselling author

Jeffrey Brown

and by ______________________

Scholastic Inc.

This page is boring . . .

www.starwars.com
Scholastic Children's Books
An imprint of Scholastic Ltd
Euston House, 24 Eversholt Street, London, NW1 1DB, UK
Registered office: Westfield Road, Southam, Warwickshire, CV47 0RA

First published in the US by Scholastic Inc, 2015
First published in the UK by Scholastic Ltd, 2015

ISBN 978 1407 16326 0

A CIP catalogue record for this book
is available from the British Library.

Printed by CPI Group (UK) Ltd, Croydon, CR0 4YY
Papers used by Scholastic Children's Books are made
from wood grown in sustainable forests.

1 3 5 7 9 10 8 6 4 2

www.scholastic.co.uk

A long time ago in a galaxy far, far away. . . .

There was a kid named

____

(that's you) who was destined to write in this book and become the GREATEST Jedi in the GALAXY. Are you ready to have some FUN?! If YES, turn the page. (If NO, close this book, and go eat your veggies.)

Hi, my name's Roan Novachez. I just graduated from Jedi Academy, and soon I'll be a super-awesome Jedi. Being a Jedi is more than just being a lightsaber-wielding knight—it's also keeping the peace throughout the galaxy. It doesn't hurt that you also get to be friends with awesome aliens, build neat-o droids, and fly really cool spaceships!
Heh heh. A Jedi Master, I am. When older you are, what do you want to do?

CREATE AN ALIEN

There are a lot of aliens in this galaxy. If you could create an alien, what would he/she/it look like? How many eyes does it have? What color is its skin? What does it eat? Is it good or bad? Use the space on the next page to draw the alien.

Stuff to know about Ewoks
Average height = one meter tall
Wear hoods, sometimes decorated with bones and feathers.
Strong sense of smell. Also, smelly when wet.
Only technology is simple wood tools and weapons.
Live on forest moon of Endor
Endor
Live in villages built of wood and mud, suspended in trees

Draw here!

Good job!

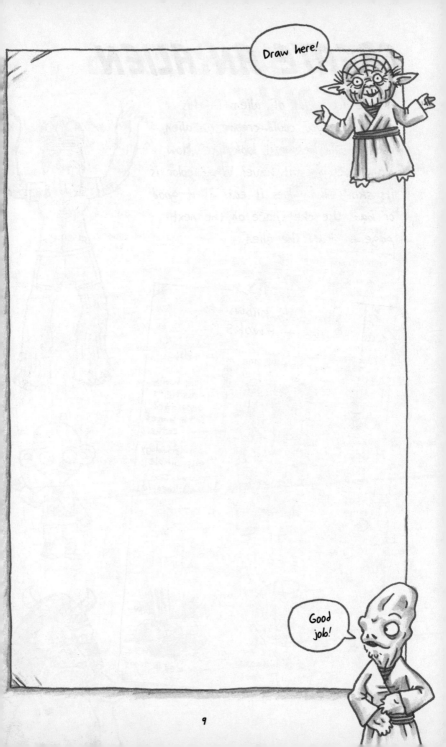

BUILD YOUR CLASS SCHEDULE

If you were invited to join Jedi Academy, wha kind of classes would you take? Dodgeball? Space-cooking? Lightsaber dueling?

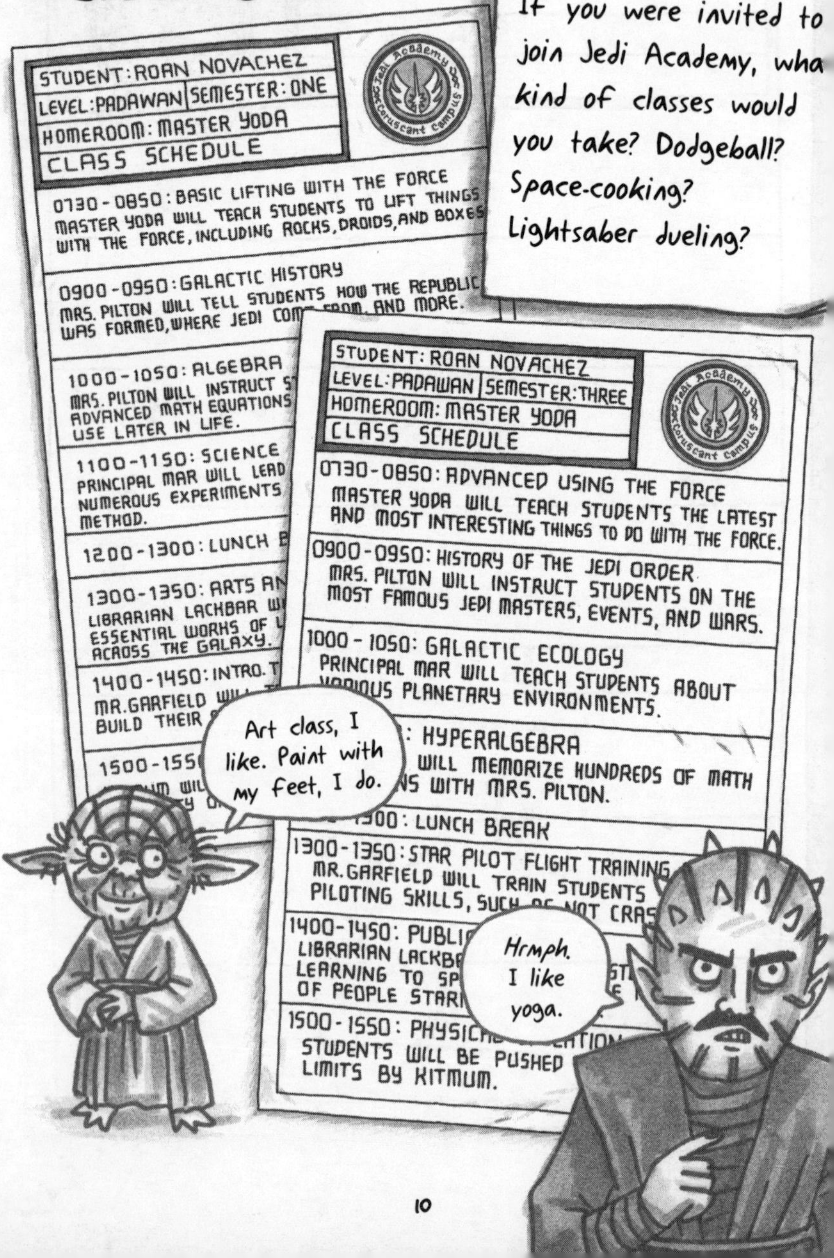

STUDENT: ROAN NOVACHEZ
LEVEL: PADAWAN
SEMESTER: ONE
HOMEROOM: MASTER YODA
CLASS SCHEDULE
Jedi Academy Coruscant Campus
0730 - 0850: BASIC LIFTING WITH THE FORCE
MASTER YODA WILL TEACH STUDENTS TO LIFT THINGS WITH THE FORCE, INCLUDING ROCKS, DROIDS, AND BOXES
0900 - 0950: GALACTIC HISTORY
MRS. PILTON WILL TELL STUDENTS HOW THE REPUBLIC WAS FORMED, WHERE JEDI COM
AND MORE.
1000 - 1050: ALGEBRA
MRS. PILTON WILL INSTRUCT
ADVANCED MATH EQUATIONS
USE LATER IN LIFE.
1100 - 1150: SCIENCE
PRINCIPAL MAR WILL LEAD
NUMEROUS EXPERIMENTS
METHOD.
1200 - 1300: LUNCH
1300 - 1350: ARTS
LIBRARIAN LACKBAR
ESSENTIAL WORKS OF
ACROSS THE GALAXY.
1400 - 1450: INTRO.
MR. GARFIELD
BUILD THEIR
1500 - 155
STUDENT: ROAN NOVACHEZ
LEVEL: PADAWAN
SEMESTER: THREE
HOMEROOM: MASTER YODA
CLASS SCHEDULE
Jedi Academy Coruscant Campus
0730 - 0850: ADVANCED USING THE FORCE
MASTER YODA WILL TEACH STUDENTS THE LATEST AND MOST INTERESTING THINGS TO DO WITH THE FORCE.
0900 - 0950: HISTORY OF THE JEDI ORDER
MRS. PILTON WILL INSTRUCT STUDENTS ON THE MOST FAMOUS JEDI MASTERS, EVENTS, AND WARS.
1000 - 1050: GALACTIC ECOLOGY
PRINCIPAL MAR WILL TEACH STUDENTS ABOUT
US PLANETARY ENVIRONMENTS.
HYPERALGEBRA
WILL MEMORIZE HUNDREDS OF MATH
NS WITH MRS. PILTON.
LUNCH BREAK
1300 - 1350: STAR PILOT FLIGHT TRAINING
MR. GARFIELD WILL TRAIN STUDENTS
PILOTING SKILLS, SUCH
NOT CRAS
1400 - 1450: PUBLI
LIBRARIAN LACKB
LEARNING TO SP
OF PEOPLE STAR
1500 - 1550: PHYSIC
STUDENTS WILL BE PUSHED
LIMITS BY KITMUM.
Art class, I like. Paint with my feet, I do.
Hrmph. I like yoga.

Jedi Academy
Coruscant Campus

DRAWING 101

Do you like to draw? A good (and easy) way to start drawing people is to use stick figures. You can add life to them with just a few simple strokes. Check out these stick figures battling with lightsabers. Now draw your own.

HMMM.
The Force is strong in your art. Keep drawing, you should.

FINISH THE COMIC

What's happening in this story? It's up to you to write what everyone is saying...

shplop!
chew
chew
chew
crunch
chew

STORY STARTER

EWOK PILOT
Yub yub!
First Issue Collector's Item!
By Roan Novachez

Roan writes and draws stories about an Ewok Pilot—a furry, funny, and often stubborn Ewok—who (kind of) flies spaceships. If you could write your own space story about a pilot, what would it be about? Here, we'll get you started, and you finish the story . . .

A long time ago, in a galaxy far, far away, there was a young kid who wanted to be a pilot. One day, this kid, named ____________________, found a spaceship behind the school. Going inside, the ship seemed to come to life. "Where do you want to go to?" the spaceship asked.

(Now you finish the story!)

Enjoying yourself, are you? Hmmm. More to come, there is.

FOOD FIGHT!

LISTS

Roan and the other Jedi Academy students got into a huge food fight. Probably because they couldn't stomach Gammy's bizarre cooking. Let's talk about you and food . . .

hop!
CUTE♡

List five disgusting things to put on a pizza for your worst enemy . . .

___

What's the WEIRDEST thing you've ever eaten?

___

What's your favorite food? Would you still eat it if it were covered in ________?

___

What would you rather eat: chocolate-covered grasshoppers or cheese-flavored mealworms?

___

Did you know on some worlds, insects and eyeballs are considered delicious? Which would you rather eat?

___

What would you rather do: eat an octopus or be eaten by an alien?

___

What do you think smells better: tauntaun or rancor?

___

CREATE YOUR OWN LIGHTSABER

One of the most powerful weapons in the universe belongs to the Jedi—a lightsaber. Each Jedi designs his or her own choosing a different crystal, color, and look. Describe what kind of lightsaber you want. Would it have one blade or two (like the Sith Lords)? What color would it be? If you don't want a lightsaber, but have another idea for a cool weapon, draw that!

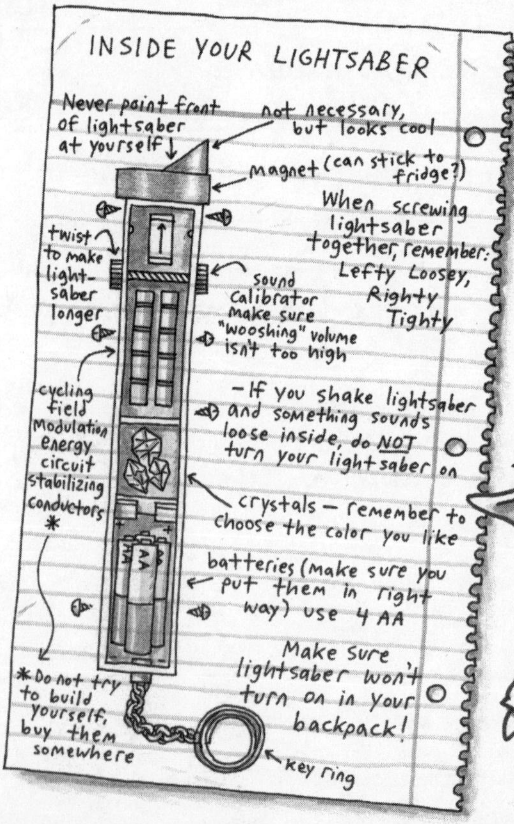
INSIDE YOUR LIGHTSABER
Never point front of lightsaber at yourself
not necessary, but looks cool
magnet (can stick to fridge?)
When screwing lightsaber together, remember: Lefty Loosey, Righty Tighty
twist to make light-saber longer
sound calibrator make sure "wooshing" volume isn't too high
- If you shake lightsaber and something sounds loose inside, do NOT turn your lightsaber on
cycling field Modulation energy circuit stabilizing conductors *
crystals – remember to choose the color you like
batteries (make sure you put them in right way) use 4 AA
AA
Make sure lightsaber won't turn on in your backpack!
* Do not try to build yourself, buy them somewhere
key ring

Remember, with your lightsaber, do not run. Or get hurt, you will.

JOURNAL

There!
Maybe I can do well in Plant School after all.
Doomed.

At the beginning of Roan's story, he was worried about going to PLANT SCHOOL, trying to get into PILOT SCHOOL, and ended up going to JEDI ACADEMY. If you could choose, which school would you go to? And why? Or, if you want, write about one of your adventures at one (or all 3) schools!

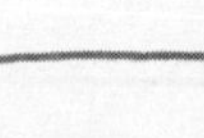

Deksh!

MAKE A ROBOT

For a school assignment, Roan and his classmates had to build a robot. Have you ever built a robot? Well, if you haven't, you should try! First though you should make the plans . . . what kind of robot would you create? Would he be made to help you, fight others, or just make pizzas?

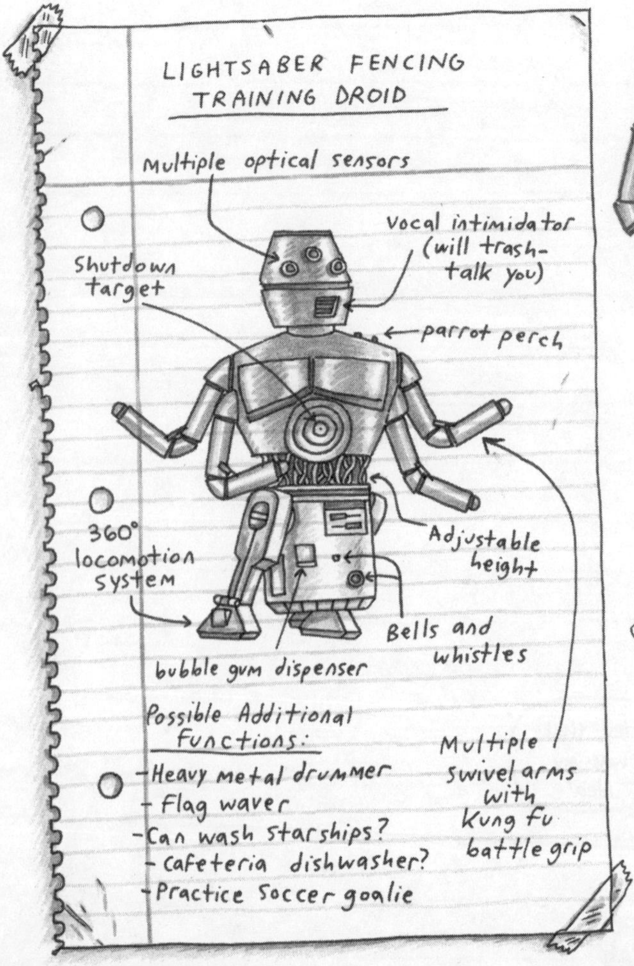

LIGHTSABER FENCING TRAINING DROID
Multiple optical sensors
Vocal intimidator (will trash-talk you)
Shutdown target
parrot perch
360° locomotion system
Adjustable height
Bells and whistles
bubble gum dispenser
Multiple swivel arms with Kung fu battle grip
Possible Additional Functions:
- Heavy metal drummer
- Flag waver
- Can wash starships?
- Cafeteria dishwasher?
- Practice soccer goalie

Hey, that was my idea!
No, it wasn't. Copycat.

HOW TO DRAW

I've always loved drawing Ewoks, and I've always loved flying, so it made sense for me to make a comic called EWOK PILOT. Here, I'll show you how to draw Ewok Pilot.

1) First, draw his face. Decide what kind of mood he is in.

2) Draw his "clothes," and add his ears.

3) Then you draw his body.

4) Last, you draw whatever is happening around him!

STORY STARTER

Jedi have all kinds of amazing abilities. They can use the Force to move or "push" things with their minds. They can jump high into the air. They can use Jedi mind tricks to persuade the weak-minded. They have lightsabers. And Sith Lords can create Force-lightning! If you could have any Force power, what would it be? Write a story about how you discover your power and what you would do with it.

Oh! I'm doing it!

KRAZAKT!

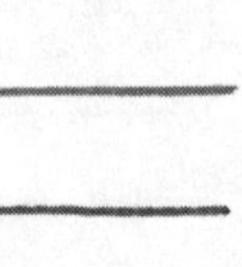

FINISH THE STORY

Reg and Jax grew up on Tatooine, just like Roan. But they went to Pilot School and have been flying all over the universe. They think they're pretty cool—though actually, they ARE pretty cool. But they're having a hard time finishing their story. Fill in the blanks with your own words to help them out.

Hey, Roan. Still stuck pretending those rocks are spaceships?
Hunh?

Reg and Jax always wanted to be the

____________________________ star pilots in

the galaxy. One day, they decided to borrow the

____________________________ and use it to fly

to the planet ____________________________.

But on their way, a bunch of bad guys called the ________________________________ came after them, wanting to steal their lunch money.

Reg and Jax forgot to arm their weapons, so they had to lose the bad guys. First, they flew into an asteroid belt. But when they tried to land, a giant ________________________________ came out of a hole and tried to ________________________________ them. Finally, they lost the bad guys. But then a bunch of space pirates came after them, wanting to take their ________________________________. They punched in the hyperdrive and zipped away.

They finally got to their destination, but once they were there, they were attacked by hundreds of female ________________________________ who wanted to cook them in their ________________________________. Reg and Jax had to get out of there fast! And they did. But that's a story for another day . . .

YODA, SPEAK LIKE!

Speak backward, some people think I do. But maybe, speak backward, it's other people who do. Hmmm. Hehehe. Try and speak like me, you should.
Actually. Do or do not. There is no try.

Things Yoda Said This Week
at peace
calm
(maybe Yoda is wrinkly from spending lots of time relaxing in hot baths!)

THINGS YODA SAID THIS WEEK

DRAW YOUR FRIENDS AS ALIENS

What if you and your friends were from different planets? What would you (and they) look like? Draw your friends as aliens. Or your parents. Or even your teachers!

INVENT A SECRET HANDSHAKE

Do you and your friends have a secret handshake? All cool people should have a secret handshake. I have, like, two hundred of them. (I just wish I had more friends to use them with . . .)

Describe your secret handshake here . . . then practice with your best friend.

JOKE TIME

Why did the angry Jedi cross the road?
To get to the dark side!
What do you call a potato that has gone to the dark side?
Vader tots!
When did Yoda suspect the evil chancellor was turning to the dark side?
In the Sith grade.
Why is a droid mechanic never lonely?
Because he's always MAKING new friends.
Why did Yoda visit the bank?
He needed a bank clone!

JOURNAL

Roan has an older brother and a younger brother. Dav likes to joke around with Roan, but he also gives him good advice. And Ollie looks up to Roan, and wants to be just like him when he gets older. Do you look up to anybody? Do you have anyone who looks up to you?

Did you check the mail yet? I'm waiting for a couple letters...
Mail? No one uses mail anymore.

Roan, how you do that?!

SPORTS AND STUFF

RRRRRAAAARRRGGHHH!!!
What Kitmum is trying to say is: At Jedi Academy, Padawans have to be in peak physical condition so they can be strong Jedi. What are some of your favorite sports? What do you like to do for fun?
Ugh. Sports are too much work for me . . . no, thanks. I like video games. What are some of your things to do for fun that don't involve running around and sweating?
Hey!
AAAUUGGHH!

STORY STARTER

Telling spooky stories around a campfire is a tradition all around the galaxy. What's the scariest story you've ever heard? Or maybe just write your own here with the space provided.

I'm glad we made it back before dark...
Why? Because it would be so hard to see?
No, because of the Ghost Wookiee!
The Ghost Wookiee is the spirit of an angry Wookiee who haunts the forests of Kashyyyk, looking for unsuspecting travelers to crush in its massive arms!

Even I think that's scary.

ALIEN PETS

Roan and Gaiana cared for a furry little voorpak from Naboo. The galaxy is filled with all kinds of weird animals and creatures and stuff. If you could have any pet alien, what would it be? What kind of adventures (and trouble) would you and your new pet get into? Write a story about it . . .

katarn

webweaver

I would get a baby rancor. Then I'd train it to eat everyone. Well, everyone except me.

MORE JOKES

Uh-oh, looks like Ronald and Cronah are at it again. Do you know any jokes? If so, write 'em down!

How do Ewoks talk over far distances?
E-Walkie talkies.
What does Jabba the Hutt eat?
Hutt dogs!
What is a Jedi's favorite toy?
A Yo-Yoda.
Which side of an Ewok has the most hair?
The outside!
How do you unlock a door on Kashyyyk?
With a Wook-key.
What do you call a man who brings dinner to a rancor?
The appetizer.

I prefer poetry:
Roses are red
Violets are blue
If you love Jedi
May the Force be with you.

STORY STARTER

It's time to write another story. I'll get you started, and then YOU finish it!

The giant robot sat up and looked around. He couldn't remember who he was or who made him. He wasn't even sure if he was a good guy or a bad guy. As he looked around the strange spaceship, he wondered where he was and how he got here. He took a step off the metal table and stood up. He was dizzy for just a moment and then everything shook violently for one second. Then everything was still. Then he realized why. The spaceship had landed. The door opened automatically. The first thing he saw was nothing but light, but then . . .

SELF-PORTRAIT

When Roan was drawing, he created several different versions of Yoda. Some of these could be called different styles of art. There's no right or wrong way to draw something, just different ones! Why don't you use the space provided to draw YOURSELF? Use a photo or a mirror, and then draw yourself in cartoon form. Remember, there's no right or wrong way to do it—just have fun!

JOURNAL

It wasn't easy for Roan to become an awesome Jedi. It took a lot of work. He had to deal with homework and friends and bullies and all kinds of crazy stuff—and at the same time, he had to read, train, and listen to his teachers. What's something in your life that you have had to practice so you can become better?

Yeha!

FINISH THE COMIC

What are they saying?

I don't know. You write their dialogue.

This is a free page. Do something awesome.

VIDEO GAMES

What are some of your favorite video games?
If you could create you own video game, what would it be about? Would it have dragons or monsters or aliens? Who would be the hero? Would there be weapons or mazes? What would it be called? Write or draw about your dream video game here.

In range...target's coming up. Almost there... bomb's away!

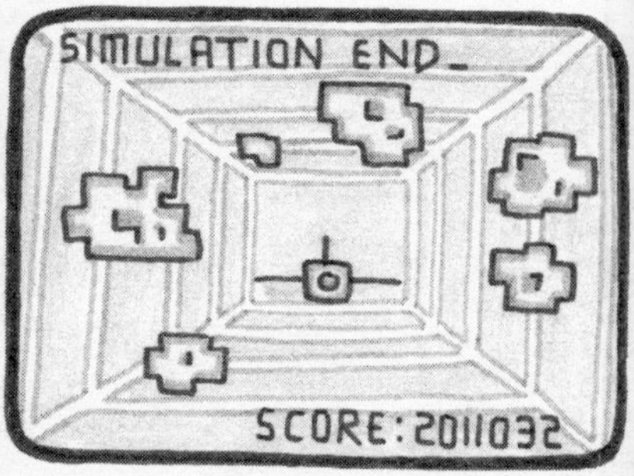
SIMULATION END_
SCORE: 2011032

1P
2P

What does this button do? Ooh!
What happened?
How do I do this?

MAZES AND LABYRINTHS

Obstacle courses and mazes are fun to do and fun to make! Design your own maze or obstacle course on the next page.

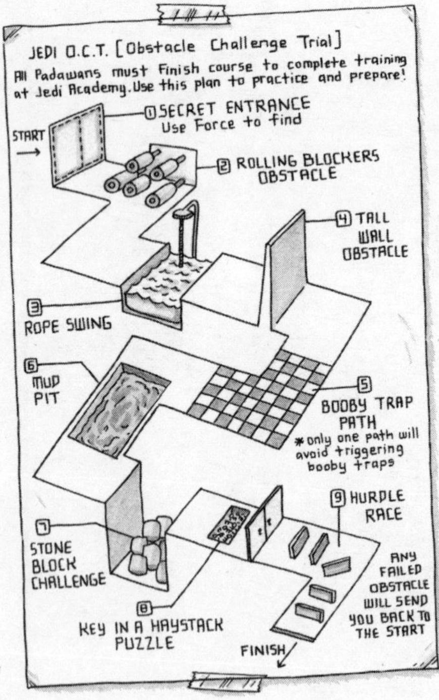

JEDI O.C.T. [Obstacle Challenge Trial]
All Padawans must Finish course to complete training at Jedi Academy. Use this plan to practice and prepare!
START
① SECRET ENTRANCE Use Force to find
② ROLLING BLOCKERS OBSTACLE
③ ROPE SWING
④ TALL WALL OBSTACLE
⑤ BOOBY TRAP PATH
* only one path will avoid triggering booby traps
⑥ MUD PIT
⑦ STONE BLOCK CHALLENGE
⑧ KEY IN A HAYSTACK PUZZLE
⑨ HURDLE RACE
ANY FAILED OBSTACLE WILL SEND YOU BACK TO THE START
FINISH

Wait, where am I?

WHAT'S GOING ON IN YOUR BRAIN?!

Roan has a LOT going on in his brain every hour that he's awake (and even when he's trying to sleep). What's going on in your brain? What do you think about the most and the least? Make a list or draw a picture like Roan's.

Think Think Think
Think Think
Think Think Think
Think Think
Think

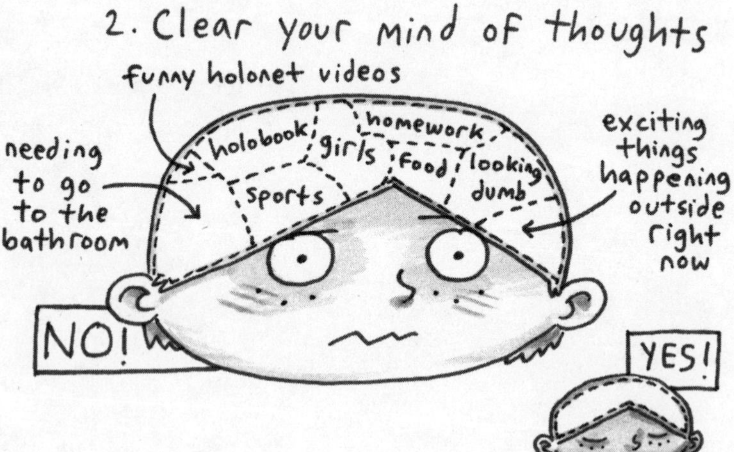
2. Clear your mind of thoughts
funny holonet videos
needing to go to the bathroom
holobook
girls
homework
sports
food
looking dumb
exciting things happening outside right now
NO!
YES!

THAT'S MORE LIKE IT.

PADAWAN OBSERVER

The Padawan Observer

Write a fake article about yourself in the Jedi Academy student newspaper. Make sure to draw pictures!

CAMPAIGN POSTER

If you ran for president of the galaxy, what would your campaign poster say and look like? Draw one here.

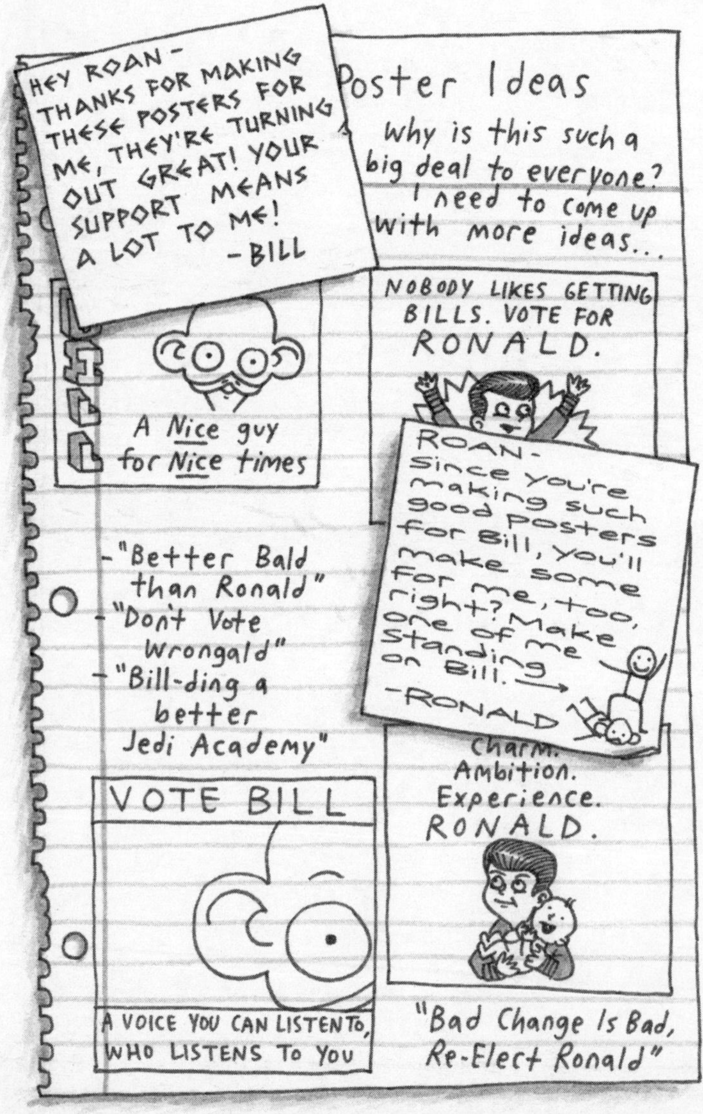
HEY ROAN-
THANKS FOR MAKING THESE POSTERS FOR ME, THEY'RE TURNING OUT GREAT! YOUR SUPPORT MEANS A LOT TO ME!
-BILL
Poster Ideas
Why is this such a big deal to everyone? I need to come up with more ideas...
BILL
A Nice guy for Nice times
NOBODY LIKES GETTING BILLS. VOTE FOR RONALD.
ROAN-
Since you're making such good posters for Bill, you'll make some for me, too, right? Make one of me standing on Bill.
-RONALD
-"Better Bald than Ronald"
-"Don't Vote Wrongald"
-"Bill-ding a better Jedi Academy"
Charm. Ambition. Experience. RONALD.
VOTE BILL
A VOICE YOU CAN LISTEN TO, WHO LISTENS TO YOU
"Bad Change Is Bad, Re-Elect Ronald"

DESIGN YOUR OWN SPACESHIP

There are all kinds of cool spaceships out in space. Ewok Pilot and Jawa Pilot both have ships (or at least they did, but they keep blowing them up!). And Roan has always wanted to be a star pilot (although Mr. G. is always making him wash ships instead of fly them). If you could be a star pilot and design your own spaceship, what would it look like? Make some sketches here!

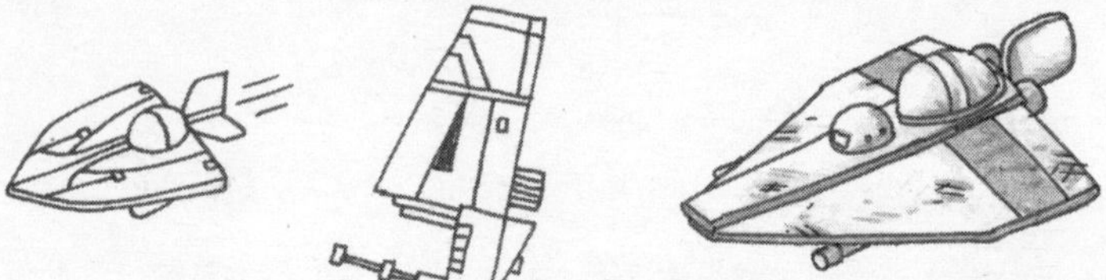

Prepare to enter hyperspace.

HMPH. YOU MISSED A SPOT HERE.

MAPS

Drawing maps is awesome. Here's a map to Pasha's house. Now you draw a map to somewhere! Maybe to school? Or a friend's house? If you can't think of a real place to draw a map, then make something up. Maybe a treasure map. Treasure is awesome, too.

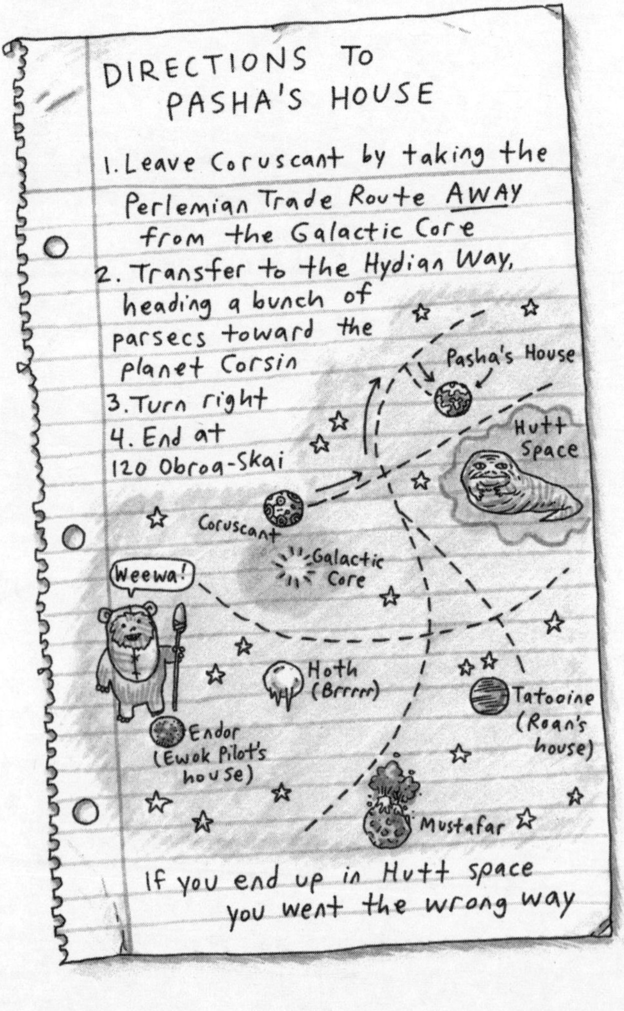

DIRECTIONS TO PASHA'S HOUSE
1. Leave Coruscant by taking the Perlemian Trade Route AWAY from the Galactic Core
2. Transfer to the Hydian Way, heading a bunch of parsecs toward the planet Corsin
3. Turn right
4. End at 120 Obroa-Skai
Pasha's House
Hutt Space
Coruscant
Galactic Core
Weewa!
Hoth (Brrrrr)
Tatooine (Roan's house)
Endor (Ewok Pilot's house)
Mustafar
If you end up in Hutt space you went the wrong way

NAPTIME

Looks like everyone fell asleep. Do whatever you want with this free space.

ZZZZZZZZZZZZZZZZZ
Oh, dear.
SNORE

JOURNAL

If you were in Roan's class, who would you hang out with? Who would be your best friend? Who would be your enemy? Who would be your favorite teacher?

The Padawan Observer End-of-the-Year Awards!
Best Student
Highest Flying
Best Friend
Most Rhythmic
Greenest
Biggest Heart
Best New Talent
Most Surprising
Most Mistaken for a Trash Can
Best Victory Dance
Least Likely to Laugh
Best Comic
Most in Need of a Haircut
Quietest
Best at Making Faces
Future Sith Lord
Toughest
Cuddliest
THE PADAWAN OBSERVER
VOL. MXIV #12

VACATIONS

Roan grew up on the desert planet Tatooine. Then he went to Coruscant, a planet that is one huge city, to attend Jedi Academy. He even visited the ice planet Hoth. What are some of the coolest (or warmest) places you've been to? What is the most remote? What is the most populated? What is the highest place you've been to? Lowest? Draw some pictures of the places you've been!

300
300
300
300
400
400
500
500
500
BILL
400
1205
200

STORY STARTER

Imagine you went to Jedi Academy. Write a story about your day there. What would it be like? What kind of trouble would you get into? What kind of fun would you have?

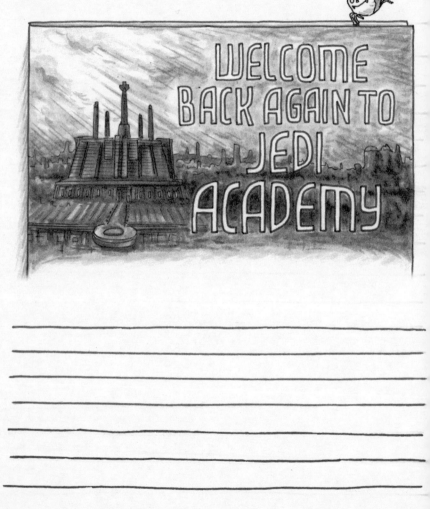

WELCOME BACK AGAIN TO JEDI ACADEMY

LISTS

If you could have a space adventure with people you know, whom would you take? Below are some spaces to fill in the people you know as space heroes (and villains)!

FIST BUMP WITH THE FORCE!

PILOT: ______________________

COPILOT: ______________________

JEDI: ______________________

JEDI MASTER: ______________________

JEDI PADAWAN: ______________________

SITH LORD: ______________________

SIDEKICK: ______________________

PRINCESS: ______________________

DROIDS: ______________________

STORY STARTER

Now write a story with the cast you created. Make sure you have fun adventures!

JOURNAL

Roan isn't a fan of bugs. Is there anything you don't like? What are you most afraid of? Don't be embarrassed, even Jedi are afraid of stuff. But they must learn to overcome their fear.

Bugs.
AAHHH! GET IT OFF! GET IT OFF!
Coo

FACE DOODLES

Ha ha ha!
Look at this one!
Hee hee!
Ha!
Ow!
Hey, what's all that noise out there?!
woof
Mah-hhh

Do you ever doodle on top of pictures? What about adding a moustache or a pair of glasses? Maybe some fangs or a funny hairdo? It's easy and fun. You try it now.

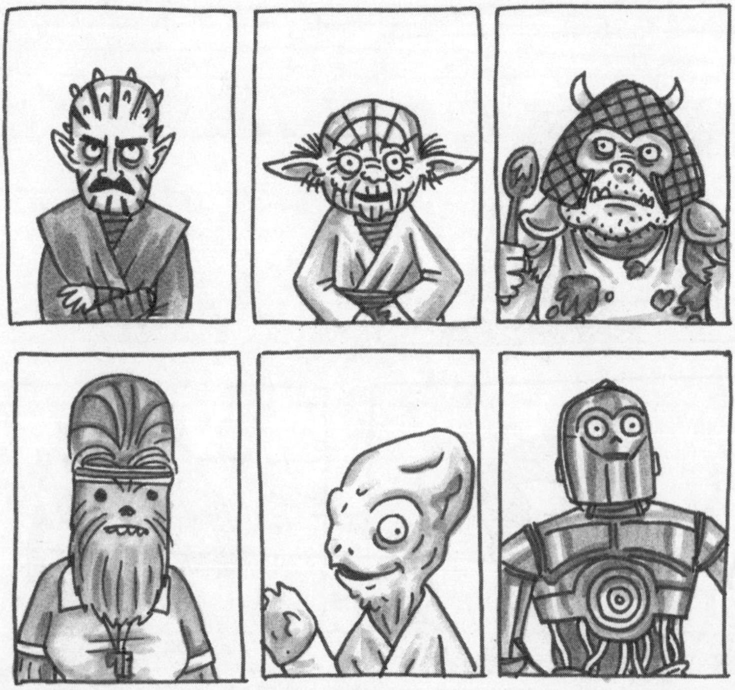

PARTY TIME!

Roan has been to lots of school dances, ice cream socials, and other kinds of parties. Kids (and aliens) like to party. If you could throw a party, what would be the theme? What kind of music would you play? Who would you invite? What would make it the coolest party ever?

LIGHT(saber) IT UP!
SCHOOL DANCE
*Don't really bring your lightsabers, that's dangerous! We'll have glow sticks
NEXT HEPTADAY @ 1900
FREE ENTRY
Brought to you by the Student Council · Ronald Rinzler, President

JOIN US FOR AN ICE CREAM SOCIAL
All-natural ice cream made by the students!
On The Jedi Academy Front Lawn. Pentaday
Presented By The Cooking Club
PLEASE DO NOT PLACE ICE CREAM ON TOP OF DROIDS

PADAWAN OBSERVER

The Padawan Observer

Write another fake article in the Jedi Academy student newspaper. It can be about whatever you want. Have fun with it!

OLLIE'S PAGES

Roan not here.
This my page now.
I draw somthin.
Ollie!

Roan- Ollie is excited for you to come home for break- he made this for you! Love, Mom
I gong be Jed i lic
Roan, that was sweet of you and your friends to send Ollie the backpack. He even took it to bed! Love, Mom
I lov My bakpak
Thanc U
I put my buks in it

Hi Roan!
Ollie wanted to send you this drawing.
I hope you're having fun in star pilot training!
Love, Mom
Dear RONe
Please come home anb pla wit h me
LUV OLLIƐ

ANIMAL DRAWING

The galaxy is filled with all kinds of wild animals. What's the coolest/weirdest/craziest animal you've seen in real life? Practice drawing it here.

STORY STARTER

Imagine you crash-landed on a strange alien planet . . . now write a story about it! Who would you meet? What would you do? How would you escape?

Have you seen Ewok Pilot?
Now he's missing, too?!
Meanwhile...
Tyeht danti
Ookwass dok pundwa keena?
Yub yub.

TEACHERS

Who is your favorite teacher at school? Who is the hardest? Write a little bit about your teachers or draw a picture of them. If you don't want to do that, then pick a teacher from Jedi Academy!

I still think Roan is a pain in my behind, but you're pretty cool. So is this book. Why don't you draw some awesome stuff on these pages?

WRITE YOUR OWN STORY

All right, here is your final test . . .Time to write your own story from scratch! You decide what happens and who the characters are!
May the Force be with you.

DRAW YOUR OWN COMIC

Time to make your own comic. There's nothing but empty panels for you to fill in with your own art, balloons, and story. Can't wait to see what you make!

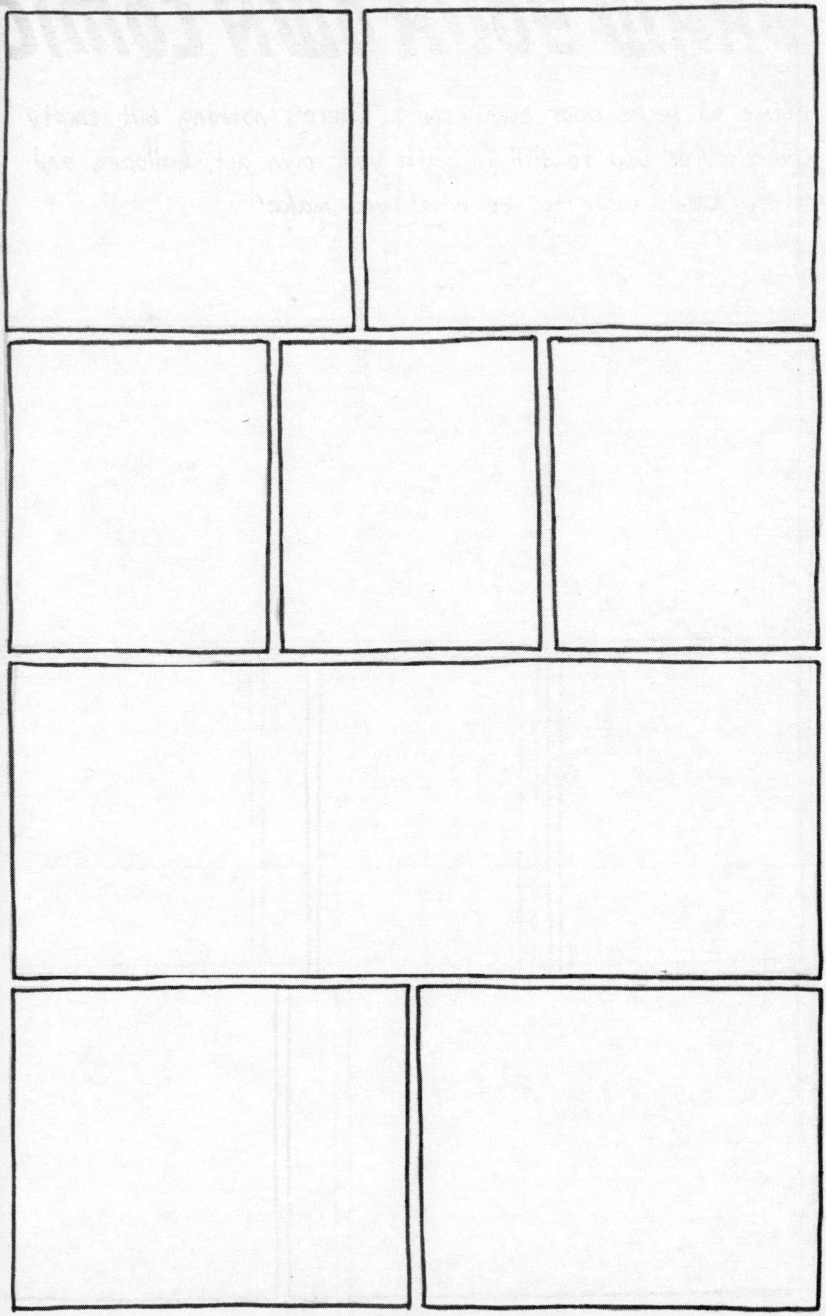

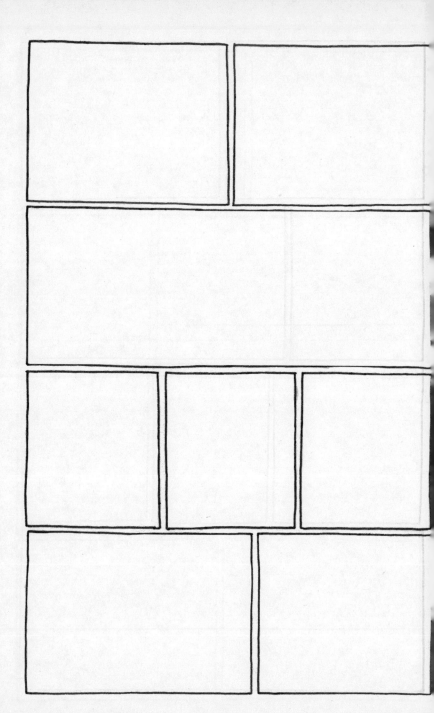

END-OF-THE-YEAR AWARDS

It's almost the end . . . I know, too bad, so sad. But make sure to fill in some of the people who inspired this book. Your friends, your family, maybe even people you don't like all that much. Then say what they're good for (or bad at)!

The Padawan Observer End-of-the-Year Awards!
Best Student
Highest Flying
Most Rhythmic
Greenest

The Padawan Observer End-of-the-Year Awards!
THE PADAWAN OBSERVER
VOL. MX
Eedada huutaveet!

VORPEE CLONE REVEAL

I guess you figured out by now that Voorpee got cloned again. Voorpaks are all over this book.
But can you count them? Go through and find every Voorpee clone. There should be ____________ of them.

Answer: 41

DIPLOMA

Write your name here. You graduated!

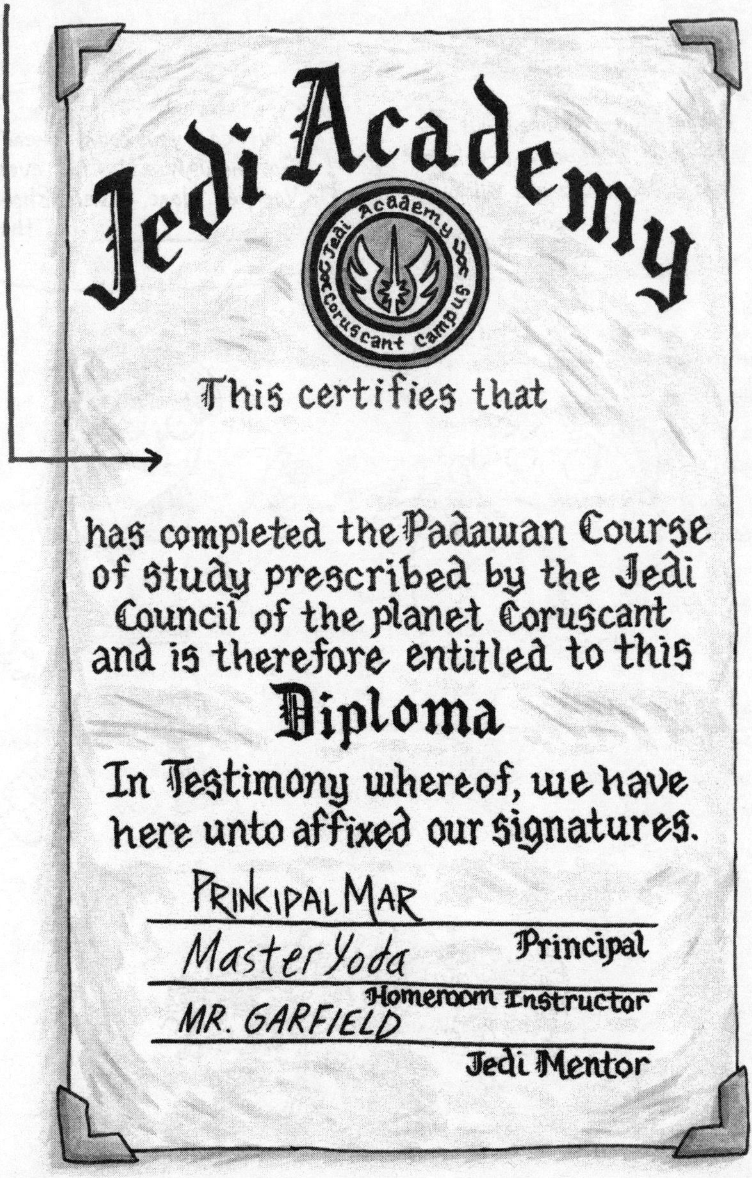

Jedi Academy
Jedi Academy Coruscant Campus
This certifies that
has completed the Padawan Course of study prescribed by the Jedi Council of the planet Coruscant and is therefore entitled to this
Diploma
In Testimony whereof, we have here unto affixed our signatures.
PRINCIPAL MAR
Principal
Master Yoda
Homeroom Instructor
MR. GARFIELD
Jedi Mentor

EWOK DICTIONARY

Ewok Pilot says some pretty hilarious stuff, doesn't he? What's that? What do you mean you don't speak Ewok?! Well, let's help you out . . . Here's some translations for you. Now you can go back through this book and translate the crazy stuff that Ewok Pilot is saying!

Acha — okay, all right

Ah-ah — water

Allayloo — celebrate

Ando — forward

Azar — magic

Bi toto — direction

Bok chuu-ock — far away

Bugdoo — hungry

Cha — them

Chaaa — this one

Chak — yes

Che womok! — Beware!

Chek — soup

Choo doo — enough

Dangar — attack

Danthee — maybe

Deksh — oh, dear/oh, my

Den — no

Drik — happy

Ee chee wa maa! — Wow, gee whiz! Oh my goodness!

Ee choya — hey

Eedada huutaveet — spaceship

Ees — we

Ehda — evil, or bad

Eyok-nee-chug — What is that?

Fudana — wait

Geetch — push

Glek — sad

Goopa — hi

Goot — good

Grenchicit — hang on/ hold on

Gunda — yummy

Gyeesh — please

Ileeay — stop

Jeerota — friend

Kaiya — giddy up!

Kush drojh? — What's going on?

Labu labu — how much?

Luka — stars

Luu — beautiful

Manna manna — food

Na-chin — tribe

Na goo — stop!

Nuv — love

Ooba — rain

Reh rehluu — dance

Roda — to eat

Sku — hello

Sunee — sun

Teeha — thank you

T'hesh — quiet

Thuk — rock

Toto — is/does

Treek — go

Tyeht danti? — What happened?

Tyehtgeethin — stranger

Uuta — sky

Weewa — home

Yaa-yaah! — Greetings

Yeha — good-bye

Yub nub — freedom

Yub yub — Let's go

Yubnub — hooray

Zeekee — safe

JAWA DICTIONARY

You don't speak Jawa, either?! It's like you're not even from this galaxy. Here, I'll help you out with a dictionary of Jawa translations, too. Make sure you go back through Jedi Academy, Return of the Padawan, and The Phantom Bully, and translate all the hilarious comics featuring Ewok Pilot and his best Jawa friend.

Ashuna – go
Ayafa – clan
Baba – days
Bazzok – cook
Bok – far
Bom'loo – bargain
Chikua – them
Dooka – junk
Eyta – friend
Gogowa – run
Gomjam – always
Ha'mfoo – burn
Hunya – enemy
Ibana – yes
Ikee – I
Ja-bo-ba – Jedi
Jubinloo – city
Kiizci – cave
Ko lopo – broken
Kurruzza – repair
Lopima – stars
Mambay – okay
M'tuske – steal
M'um m'aloo – greetings, hello
Neta – no
Okka – up
Oko – cold
Opakwa – spare parts
Ratapa – knife
Reve – ship
Rubac – rust
Sabioto – stop
Shanay – sleep
Shootogawa – shoot, blast
Sooga – food
Taa baa – thank you
Tando – fix
Theek – run
Toineepa – credit
Ton ton – sand
Ubanya – good day, good-bye
Umka – walk
Utinni – Wow! Come here. Also, a common battle cry.
Waff-mla – dessert
Wass – hot
Ysas – equal
Yuyu – right

Here are some common Jawa phrases:

Utto nye usabia atoonyoba? – Want to buy used droid?

A beton nya mombay m'bwa! – This is mine, all mine!

Ookwas dok pundwa keena? – Where is the nearest fuel station?

Etee uwanna waa. – I want to trade.

ABOUT THE AUTHOR
(THAT'S YOU!)

This is the part where you say something cool about yourself. Imagine if you had to sum yourself up in 2-3 sentences, what would you say? Draw yourself if you want, too. For inspiration, look at the last page of the Jedi Academy books and see how Jeffrey Brown did it.

JAWA DICTIONARY

You don't speak Jawa, either?! It's like you're not even from this galaxy. Here, I'll help you out with a dictionary of Jawa translations, too. Make sure you go back through Jedi Academy, Return of the Padawan, and The Phantom Bully, and translate all the hilarious comics featuring Ewok Pilot and his best Jawa friend.

Ashuna – go

Ayafa – clan

Baba – days

Bazzok – cook

Bok – far

Bom'loo – bargain

Chikua – them

Dooka – junk

Eyta – friend

Gogowa – run

Gomjam – always

Ha'mfoo – burn

Hunya – enemy

Ibana – yes

Ikee – I

Ja-bo-ba – Jedi

Jubinloo – city

Kiizci – cave

Ko lopo – broken

Kurruzza – repair

Lopima – stars

Mambay – okay

M'tuske – steal

M'um m'aloo – greetings, hello

Neta – no

Okka – up

Oko – cold

Opakwa – spare parts

Ratapa – knife

Reve – ship

Rubac – rust

Sabioto – stop

Shanay – sleep

Shootogawa – shoot, blast

Sooga – food

Taa baa – thank you

Tando – fix

Theek – run

Toineepa – credit

Ton ton – sand

Ubanya – good day, good-bye

Umka – walk

Utinni – Wow! Come here. Also, a common battle cry.

Waff-mla – dessert

Wass – hot

Ysas – equal

Yuyu – right

Here are some common Jawa phrases:

Utto nye usabia atoonyoba? – Want to buy used droid?

A beton nya mombay m'bwa! – This is mine, all mine!

Ookwas dok pundwa keena? – Where is the nearest fuel station?

Etee uwanna waa. – I want to trade.

ABOUT THE AUTHOR (THAT'S YOU!)

This is the part where you say something cool about yourself. Imagine if you had to sum yourself up in 2-3 sentences, what would you say? Draw yourself if you want, too. For inspiration, look at the last page of the Jedi Academy books and see how Jeffrey Brown did it.

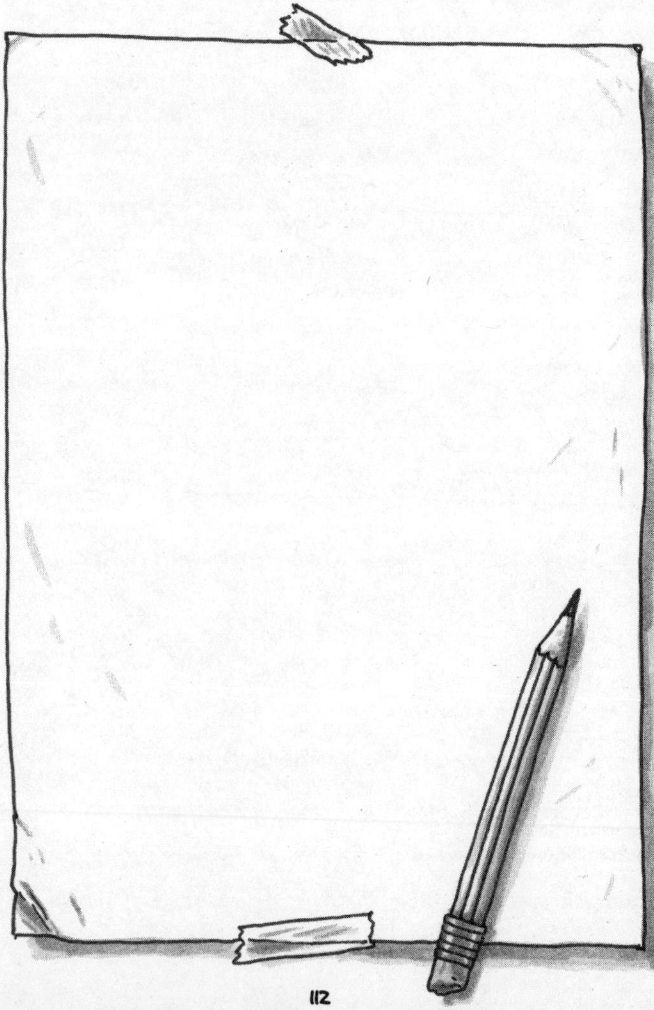